TO:

Daddy,
like splashing in puddles with our feet.
You're big and strong, with hugs that can't be beat.

Saying "I love you, Daddy" brings a smile so wide.
Let's turn the page and read side by side!

FROM:

The morning birds wake us together at dawn.
"Daddy, I love you," I sleepily yawn.

We giggle and splash as we play in the pool.
I love that my friends think my daddy's so cool!

If I prick my paw
and I'm starting to cry,
you say, "There, there, little one.
I'll dry your eyes."

We leap in the air, and we roll on the ground.
You're the best daddy and best friend around.

I love the adventures we go on together.
I'll always remember them, now and forever.

I nip at your ears but you don't really mind.
You just smile and laugh. You're always so kind!

I love you, Daddy.
You're brave and strong, too.
I can't wait to grow up
to be just like you!

My Name:
_____

My Dad's Name:
_____

My dad is the best:
_____

Together, we love to play...
_____

Daddy, I love it when you...

_____

A Picture of My Dad and Me

ISBN 978-1-968248-10-9
Written by Stephanie Moss
Illustrated by Kathryn Inkson

Designed by Hannah George
Edited by Hannah Campling

Copyright © 2021 Igloo Books Ltd

Published in 2024
First published in the UK by Igloo Books Ltd
An imprint of Igloo Books Ltd
Cottage Farm, NN6 0BJ, UK
Owned by Bonnier Books
Sveavägen 56, Stockholm, Sweden

All rights reserved, including the right of reproductionin whole or in part in any form.

IglooBooks.com
bonnierbooks.co.uk

Printed and bound in the United States of America.
10 9 8 7 6 5 4 3 2 1

Storybook Greetings® is a registered trademark of Frederic Thomas USA, Inc.
Adapted from the original for Storybook Greetings® by
Frederic Thomas USA, Inc. Naples, FL 34119
Tel: 239-593-8000 | www.fredericthomasusa.com

Send a greeting that will last a lifetime!

$8.99
ISBN 978-1-968248-10-9